Contents

Maximus Mouse

Maximus is a perfectly ordinary mouse who happens to live in St Michael's Church. He likes to think that he looks after the church and he keeps his bed and all his other belongings in the vestry. The vestry is the small room where the vicar, who really looks after the church, changes for services. Maximus eats candlewax and hymnbooks and sometimes the filling from hassocks, which are those heavy cushions that people kneel on in some churches, when they pray.

Maximus has a special mouse friend called Patrick whom you will meet later in one of these stories. Several other animals live close to Maximus and join in some of his adventures.

Maximus first popped out of the vestry when I wanted to tell some children about the Lord's Prayer. The children got to know Maximus quite well and after we had finished the first six stories they wanted to hear more about his adventures. Some mothers began to knit little woollen Maximuses and I have got one here helping me to spell words mousically. Some friends of mine have read the stories at home as well as hearing them at school.

I would like to thank the children of the Bishop Wilson School for their encouragement to write the stories and Patricia for lots of good ideas.

Brian Ogden

MAXIMUS MOUSE

Brian Ogden

Illustrated by Elke Counsell

Scripture Union
130 City Road, London EC1V 2NJ.

By the same author:
Maximus Rides Again

© Brian Ogden 1991
First published 1991
Reprinted 1992, 1993, 1995

ISBN 0 86201 680 0

Phototypeset by Input Typesetting Ltd, London
Printed and bound in Great Britain by Cox & Wyman Ltd,
Reading, Berkshire

Our Father, who art in heaven, hallowed be thy name

As the seasons turn from autumn to winter, Maximus always starts to collect paper hankies. During the week, when there are no services in St Michael's Church, it can get quite cold. Maximus likes to make a nice warm bed out of anything he can find. Hankies are best for this. He sticks two together and then stuffs them with screwed up pages from a hymn book. Humans call this a duvet but for Maximus it serves two purposes, it keeps him warm and when he wakes up he can have breakfast of bed.

During Sunday services he scampers quietly about hoping that someone will drop a hanky on the floor. One Sunday, as the people were praying, Maximus spotted a large white hanky lying on the floor near the organ. He knew it was safest to run about in hymns so people couldn't hear him. While he waited for the prayer to end he started to listen to what was being said.

Maximus, being a well brought up church mouse, put his front paws together. He knew that the people were talking to God and he heard them say 'Our Father, who art in heaven, Harold be thy name.'

He could not believe his furry ears – Harold the hedgehog was God! Surely not – he was only an ordinary sort of hedgehog, nice enough, but not the God that the humans talked to in church. But they had said 'Harold be thy name' when they were talking about God. Then the vicar started speaking and Maximus, who had forgotten the handkerchief when he heard about Harold, had to stay still and listen.

'The friends of Jesus,' said the vicar, 'once asked him to teach them to pray. "When you pray," replied Jesus, 'say "our Father, who art in heaven, hallowed be thy name." '

The vicar told all the people that they should think of God like a good father – one who loves us, cares about us, and always knows what is best for us. We should do what he tells us to do. But, if we do something which we know is wrong, he will still love us. If we are sorry then he will forgive us.

'This father,' said the vicar, 'lives in what we call heaven. That is a wonderful place where everyone is happy and no one is ill. It is the place where we go when we have finished here on earth if we love God.'

'God's name is very special,' the Vicar went on, 'it is a holy name. We should only use it when we are speaking to God or talking about God. God's name is not something to say when things go wrong. God's name is. . . .'

'Wait for it,' thought Maximus. 'I know. His name is Harold.'

'Is hallowed,' said the vicar. 'Hallowed means holy and precious.'

'Oh dear,' thought Maximus. 'I've got it all wrong again. It isn't Harold after all.'

That afternoon he went out into the churchyard and shared the joke with Harold. The little hedgehog thought it was very funny.

Heavenly Father,
Help us never to use your name wrongly but always to respect it and keep it holy. Amen

Thy kingdom come; thy will be done; on earth as it is in heaven

Maximus was dreaming in bed one morning when he was woken up by a loud knocking on the vestry door. He struggled out of his hanky duvet and scampered over to open the door. It was the postman.

'I have an important letter for you, Maximus,' said Albert the octopus. Albert made a good postman because he could sort out all the letters quickly with his eight tentacles.

'Oh,' said Maximus who was rather surprised. 'I don't get many important letters. It can't be the Church Secretary because I've paid the rent.'

Maximus said a hurried farewell to Albert and ran with the letter back to bed. He tore open the envelope and pulled out the important looking letter. It was from Foot, Foot, Foot and Mouth: Solicitors.

Dear Mr Maximus Mouse,
I regret to inform you that your great Uncle Tomouse has died. Please come to these offices for the reading of his will next Monday at 10.00 a.m.
Yours faithfully,
A. Foot.

Maximus was up early and soon found his way to Foot, Foot, Foot and Mouth: Solicitors. He was shown into a large room and was pleased to see lots of members of the family that he had not met for a long time. There were dozens of cousins, numbers of nephews, several sisters and bags of brothers. They all went silent when Mr Foot stood up to speak.

'This is the last will and testament of Tomouse,' he read. 'I, Tomouse, being of sound mind do bequeath to all my nephews cheese for one year, in equal portions.'

There were other gifts from Uncle Tomouse's will but Maximus did not hear them. He was dreaming of all that lovely cheese – a whole year's supply. Good old Uncle Tomouse. He said goodbye to all his relations and went back home to the church.

The following Sunday Maximus was in church once again for the morning service. Last week he had learned that God was like a father and that his name was holy. He wondered what he would hear today.

'Thy kingdom come, thy will be done, on earth as it is in heaven,' announced the vicar.

'Bless my tail and whiskers,' said Maximus. 'The vicar is going to read a will. Perhaps we shall all get something.'

'The kingdom of God can only come when we all do the will of God,' said the vicar. 'To do the will of God is to do what he wants; to love him and love everybody we know. We should be kind and thoughtful and think of other people before we think about ourselves. That is the will of God. Those who have finished their lives here on earth go to heaven if they love God. In heaven everyone does what God wants because they love him. On earth we have to try every day to do his will. Then we help God to make the kingdom of earth more like the kingdom of heaven.'

Maximus scratched his head with his left front paw and thought about what the vicar had said. He scuttled away as the people sang the last hymn and had a delicious hassock and cheese sandwich for lunch.

Heavenly Father,
We know that what you want us to do is what is best for our lives. Help us to know your will and give us the courage to do it. Amen

Give us this day our daily bread

Maximus was having an afternoon nap curled up in a small furry ball. He was lying in a pool of sunshine which was streaming in through the church window.

He had been very busy that morning making a new duvet from a nice hanky which the organist had dropped at choir practice. He had to make a new one as he had eaten the old one when he woke up hungry in the night. Just as he was dreaming of a large pile of hassock and cheese sandwiches there was a loud noise. He jumped up, rubbed his eyes with his front paws, and scuttled under a chair.

Several people had come into the back of the church with some large pieces of card and strips of metal. Maximus watched as they slotted the strips together and placed the large cards on them. After a while the people went away and Maximus scampered down the church to see what this strange looking thing was. On the cards were large photographs. They showed some very poor people in another country. These people seemed to be very hungry and their clothes were not much more than rags.

One of the children in a photograph was holding a bowl. Maximus read the words printed at the bottom, 'Give us this day our daily bread.' He stroked his whiskers with his front paws. He had heard the vicar talk about helping others and how the church tried to give money and pray for people who were starving. Maximus had never seen a photograph of hungry children before and he felt very sorry for them.

Just as he was thinking how dreadful it was to be so hungry he heard a strange noise coming from the vestry. As he arrived at the vestry door he saw the front half of another mouse coming through his crack in the plaster.

'Stay right there!' shouted Maximus, sounding much braver than he felt. 'What do you think you are doing coming into my church?'

'Please,' begged the other mouse. 'Please let me in.'

'All right,' said Maximus. 'Come in, but no funny tricks.'

The strange mouse pulled himself through the hole in the plaster and dropped down onto the floor of the vestry.

'Is that candlewax and cheese pie I can smell?' he asked.

Maximus saw how cold and wet and hungry he looked. Instead of being frightened of this stranger he began to feel very sorry for him. Maximus soon discovered that his new friend was called Patrick. Patrick had been living in a very old house just down the road. It was owned by an elderly lady but she had gone into a special home when she could no longer look after herself. The council had come along and knocked down her house to build a new road. Patrick and his family had nowhere to live and had lost all their clothes and

furniture and food.

Patrick had left his family sheltering under a hedge in the rain whilst he went in search of food and somewhere to live. Maximus quickly warmed up some candlewax and cheese pie. Patrick ate it noisily, wiping his whiskers with his paws, and soon finished a very large helping.

Maximus and Patrick then had a long chat about how to help the family. They decided that the best thing to do was to move into the church whilst the weather was bad. Maximus showed Patrick the Sunday School cupboard where all the drawing paper, crayons, felt pens and lesson books were kept. Patrick thought that they would be very happy in there and that his children might enjoy reading some of the stories in the lesson books. He went off to get the family and they were soon settled comfortably in the Sunday School cupboard.

The next Sunday morning the vicar said he was going to speak about another part of the Lord's Prayer.

' "Give us this day our daily bread." Most of us,' he said, 'don't have to think about our daily bread. We take it for granted that we will have more than enough to eat. At the end of the day we expect to go to bed full and not hungry. In many parts of the world where people are hungry these words are really a prayer asking God to give food. It is our duty as Christians to care about those who do not have enough to eat. We must give our prayers and our money to help. Sometimes we can care for those who live near us by making friends with them and doing practical things to help.'

Maximus rubbed his eyes and nearly shouted out, 'That's what I've done. I helped Patrick and his family.' Just in time he remembered to whisper it to himself. He cooked a very special meal that evening of hymnbook hotpot. Then he took it over to Patrick and his family and watched them eat it all up.

Heavenly Father,
Thank you for all the good things you give us, our
health, our homes, our food and our friends. We are
sorry that so often we take them all for granted. Help
us to understand what it is to need these things and give
us the love to provide them for others. Amen

*And forgive us our trespasses, as we forgive
them that trespass against us*

Maximus loved music. He could sit and eat it for hours.
Sometimes he fried it and sometimes he baked it and
sometimes he just ate it raw. He also liked to listen to
music. When the organist came into the church to prac-
tise, Maximus would sit happily listening to the hymns
for the coming Sunday. Sometimes Maximus would join
in, with the organist, on his mouseorgan.

The church had a very old organ and, from time to
time, there were some strange noises in the middle of
the hymns. A special organ repair man came to look at
it and spoke to the vicar and the organist.

'I'm afraid there is nothing we can do. It is just too
old to repair. You will have to buy a new one.'

Several months later the new organ was brought into
the church and fitted carefully into place. The organist
played some hymns to the vicar on the new organ and
they both thought that it was so much better than the
old one. There were no strange noises any more and
the organist was very happy as he looked forward to
the following Sunday.

The next night Maximus decided to explore the new organ. He could see quite well because the moon was shining in through the window of the church. He climbed the north face of the keyboard and soon found a mouse sized hole. Inside, the organ was very different from the old one. Everything was electronic with hundreds of brightly covered wires. Maximus scampered all over it, sliding down one wire, nibbling through another, and even swopping some over. It was much more exciting than the old organ, he thought. He enjoyed himself so much that he could not wait to come again. He scampered back to the vestry and was soon asleep under his handkerchief duvet after the busy night.

Just as Maximus was dreaming about showing Patrick the new organ he was woken up by the sound of voices. The vicar and the choirboys came into the vestry to get ready for the morning service. Maximus heard them talking about the new organ and how nice it would be singing to it rather than waiting for the funny noises to come. Maximus followed them all into the church. The vicar announced the first hymn. The organist placed his fingers on the keys. There was the most dreadful noise, nothing at all like a hymn tune.

It was then that Maximus realised what he had done. He had changed the wires around so much inside the organ that it could not be used. The poor vicar had to get a repair man from the organ firm to come and put it right.

Back in the vestry after the service, which had been rather spoiled without the organ, Maximus decided that he would go back to sleep again. He went over to the corner where he kept his duvet rolled up. It wasn't there. He searched everywhere for it, in the cupboards, under the carpet, and even in the waste paper basket in case

the vicar had thrown it away. He couldn't see it anywhere so he went to see Patrick in the Sunday School cupboard. Just as he reached the cupboard he saw Patrick unrolling a duvet.

'That's my duvet,' he said angrily. 'You've stolen my bed.'

'I didn't think you would mind,' said Patrick. 'You see my wife is ill and I need to keep her warm.'

'Well, you might have asked, but since you need it I will forgive you. Next time ask me if you want anything.'

Next Sunday morning the vicar continued his talks about the Lord's Prayer.

'Forgive us our trespasses as we forgive them that trespass against us,' he said. 'Trespass is an old word meaning sin or the things which we do wrong. For example, last Sunday, we had great difficulty with our new organ. It seems that someone small, like our church mouse, got inside it and re-arranged the wires. This was a wrong thing to do and it has caused us a lot of trouble. But we forgive him for doing this, providing he never does it again.'

Maximus was very ashamed at hearing this. He was really sorry for what he had done. Then he thought about Patrick and the duvet. He was glad that he had forgiven Patrick for taking the duvet and that he had been forgiven for spoiling the new organ. He sat and enjoyed listening to the organ and everyone joined in the hymns without wondering if there would be a funny noise.

Heavenly Father,
We so often ask you for forgiveness but we are not good at forgiving those who have hurt us. Help us to forgive others and always to know that you forgive us when we are really sorry. Amen

And lead us not into temptation; but deliver us from evil

You may have guessed by now that Maximus is a rather greedy mouse. You have heard quite a lot about what he eats. Hassock and cheese sandwiches, wax waffles and music muesli are all favourite items on his menu.

But Maximus is not the only one who likes his food. I have to tell you that the vicar of St Michael's Church is also very fond of certain things to eat. Mrs Vicar gets very cross with the vicar on occasions and tells him that he must lose weight or he will not get into his cassock. The cassock is the long black sort of dressing gown which vicars wear so that the people cannot see their knees knocking when they are nervous. Mrs Vicar had told her husband that he must not eat any more sweets. The vicar loved sweets but his real special treat was fudge. He adored fudge; fudge with nuts, fudge with ginger, fudge with rum and raisins, chocolate fudge, in fact any sort of fudge.

One Christmas, the church organist, who knew how much the vicar liked it, gave him a nice fat box of nut and ginger fudge. The vicar was afraid that Mrs Vicar would find it and give it to the choir boys. Instead of taking it home he popped it into the drawer in the vestry where he kept all his special bits and pieces. Sometimes, before a service, the vicar would secretly take out a piece of fudge and chew it when he thought no one was watching.

One Sunday morning Maximus was snuggled down in his duvet wondering if the music of 'Fight the good fight', which he had just eaten for breakfast, would give him tummy ache. He happened to look up just as the vicar dropped a small piece of ginger fudge into his mouth. Maximus made a note to remember what he saw and went back to sleep again.

Later that morning, after all the choirboys and the vicar had gone home, Maximus started to search the drawers for the fudge. Mice are very good at finding things that have a strong smell and he knew exactly where he would find the fudge. He pushed aside two old hymn books, a stack of out of date notices and one half of a pair of woolly gloves that had been left in church. The end of the packet was open and Maximus started to nibble a delicious piece of ginger fudge.

Just as he was thinking of moving onto a slice of nut fudge the door burst open and in came the vicar. He had come back for a hymn book for the evening service. Fortunately he didn't see Maximus, who was lying as still as he could, pretending to be a furry glove. Maximus was so frightened that he jumped down out of the drawer and ran, as fast as his little paws could manage, to hide under the old carpet in the corner. He decided against fudge for lunch and was just glad not to have been caught.

The following Sunday morning the vicar told the people that he had come to the words 'lead us not into temptation but deliver us from evil,' in the Lord's Prayer.

'This is an asking prayer,' he said. 'We are asking God that we are not tempted to do something wrong. Sometimes we want to do things which we know are wrong – this wanting is what we call temptation. We are asking God to help us not to give in to this wanting. 'Deliver us from evil' is also an asking prayer. We ask God to stop anything bad from happening to us. So these two parts of the Lord's Prayer are actually small prayers for ourselves – that we don't do wrong things and that wrong things don't happen to us.'

Maximus, who had been listening from the vestry door, suddenly thought of what had happened last Sunday morning. He had been tempted to eat the vicar's fudge and had been nearly caught doing so by the vicar.

'I think that prayer is the right one for me,' said Maximus to himself, 'lead me not into temptation but deliver me from evil. I must leave the fudge for the vicar, but I hope he doesn't get too fat.'

Heavenly Father,
Help us to know what is wrong and to do what is right
so that we may be true friends of yours. Amen

For thine is the kingdom, the power and the glory, for ever and ever. Amen

Maximus hated official looking forms – they always seemed to give him a headache. Every now and again, Albert the octopus, who, you remember, was the postman, would bring him another form to fill in. Maximus would sit and look at them and hope that they would go away. Sooner or later, though, he had to fill them in and it always took him ages.

One morning, as Maximus was lying in bed, he heard a letter flop onto the floor of the vestry. He got out of his duvet and groaned when he saw the colour of the envelope. It was light brown. Maximus knew that light brown envelopes always had forms in them.

'It's not going to be a good day,' moaned Maximus to the vestry wall. 'In fact, it's going to be a really boring day. I *hate* forms.'

Maximus threw the brown envelope down on the floor and went off to find some breakfast. He banged the vestry door behind him and scampered around in the church hoping to find a nice piece of music to eat. After a long search he found an old hymnbook near the organ and helped himself to a good meal. There was no sign of Patrick in the church so Maximus went over to the Sunday School cupboard to find him.

When he opened the cupboard door he could see that Patrick had got one of the Sunday School pencils in his paw and was writing.

'Sorry, can't come just at the moment,' said Patrick. 'I've got this census form to fill in.'

'Oh, I had one of those horrid things,' said Maximus. 'Not going to waste my time filling it in.'

'But you've got to,' replied Patrick, 'it's come from the Mouse of Commons. Every mouse must fill one in and send it back. They want to know all about you. Tell you what. If you like, when I've finished mine, I'll come and help you.'

Later that morning Patrick explained to Maximus that every few years every mouse in the country had to fill in a census form. The Mouse of Commons needed to know all about everyone – when they were born, where they lived, what work they did, and lots more. Between them they soon managed to answer all the questions on the form.

'Now they will know as much about me as I know about myself,' said Maximus.

The two friends folded up the forms and took them off to the post box. Maximus felt very pleased that he had got the job finished and thanked Patrick for his help.

The following Sunday morning Maximus was up early. He was anxious not to miss the vicar's talk as it was to be the last one about the Lord's Prayer. He found a nice warm spot near one of the radiators in the church, joined in the hymns, and settled down to listen to the vicar.

'We have come to the last part of the Lord's Prayer

today,' said the vicar. ' "For thine is the kingdom, the power and the glory, forever and ever. Amen." At the beginning of this prayer we learned about God being our father. At the end we learn even more about him. The kingdom that matters is God's kingdom in which everyone does what God wants. God is all powerful – he made us and he made the world. He is wonderful and we praise and thank him for what he is when we say he is glorious. God is so much greater than we can imagine. There has never been a time without God and there never will be – he is for ever and ever. And then finally we say Amen which means "so be it." Whenever we use the word "Amen" we are saying that we agree, that we will do what the prayer asks.'

Maximus thought about the census form that he had filled in. 'It's a bit like that. I have written down a lot about myself so someone now knows all about me. Jesus gave his friends the Lord's Prayer to use and now we all know a lot more about God. I must go and tell Patrick all about it.'

Heavenly Father,
You are greater than we can possibly understand yet your love for us is that of a father for his children. Help us to show, by the way we live, that we are members of your kingdom here on earth. Amen

Maximus has a Christmas dream

Poor Maximus was feeling tired. It was Christmas Day and he had been very busy. On Christmas Eve a lot of people had come to the church to give the building a really good clean and get it ready for Christmas. Maximus had helped by picking up all the flower petals and leaves that were lying on the floor. Unfortunately he had stood in the way of some spray polish and kept sneezing for half an hour afterwards.

He had gone to bed nice and early on Christmas Eve and hung up his stocking near his bed in the vestry. What he had forgotten was the midnight service. Just when he was settling down to sleep, covered up by a pink handkerchief duvet, the light in the vestry was put on and in came the vicar and choirboys. They were excited and talking about what presents they would have to open the next day. It was nearly one o'clock in the morning before the church was quiet again but to Maximus it seemed like no time at all before the vicar was back for the eight o'clock service and then again for the Family Service at ten thirty.

Only when the final Happy Christmases had been said and everyone had gone home for turkey and Christmas pudding could Maximus get his lunch. He had noticed that during the Family Service one of the children had dropped a carol sheet behind the radiator in the church just by the Christmas crib set.

'Just what I like for Christmas dinner,' he said to the empty church, 'cooked carol burgers.' He started with 'Good King Wencesmouse looked out' and for pudding he had three verses of 'As with gladness mice of old.' By this time, after his disturbed night and large lunch, Maximus was beginning to feel very sleepy. He climbed up into the crib and in no time at all he was fast asleep in the straw next to the baby Jesus.

Soon he was dreaming. Somehow the crib set seemed to come alive. There was the stable with the straw on the floor, there was the manger, and from it came the sound of a baby gurgling. Standing next to the baby was Joseph looking so pleased and by him was Mary looking tired but very happy. He could see some animals in the stable. A cow had just given some milk for the family to drink. A donkey and a horse were standing against the holes in the stable wall to keep cold draughts from blowing on the baby. The innkeeper's dog was on guard by the door to stop anyone disturbing the family.

Mary and Joseph lay down on the straw covered floor and soon Mary was fast asleep. In a few moments Joseph, too, had fallen asleep, leaving the animals to look after everything.

When it was very quiet, Maximus saw in his dream a small furry mouse come out of his hole in the wall. The mouse looked around at all the animals, he saw Mary and Joseph were asleep, and he scampered silently over to the manger. The soft blanket which was keeping

Jesus warm had slipped off and he was getting cold. Slowly and very quietly the little mouse picked up pieces of warm straw and covered the baby again. The mouse had one more look around and then went back to his home in the wall. Mary and Joseph never knew how the straw got there.

Maximus grunted in his sleep and thought to himself that even the smallest of us can do something to help Jesus.

Heavenly Father,
Thank you for the birth of Jesus into the world. Just as you care about us, so help us to care about other people, and do what we can for them. Amen

Maximus and the Wise Men

Maximus had a very good Christmas. It was a time when he usually ate far too much. One reason for this was that the church always had a service at Christmas called Carols by Candlelight. At this service the church was lit only by candles and each candle left a little heap of wax when it melted. No one felt like clearing it up and so it was left for several days. Maximus didn't mind at all as wax waffles were one of his favourite foods. So for a week or so after the carol service Maximus used to wander around the church searching for little piles of wax. The vicar and the church cleaner could never understand how the building got so clean without anyone doing it.

It was usually quiet after the Christmas services and before the children went back to school. The vicar had a few days holiday, the choirboys played with their Christmas presents, even Johann Sebastian, the organist's cat, was at home watching Tom and Jerry cartoons on television.

Maximus was beginning to think that he had eaten

quite enough wax waffles and it would be good to go back to hymnburgers again. He was having a last look around the crib for a specially tasty coloured wax blob when he noticed something very strange. He could see Mary and Joseph and the baby Jesus, the shepherds were there, one of them holding a lamb, but surely there should have been something else? What was missing?

Just at that moment the vestry door opened and in came the vicar with a couple of the choirboys.

'We must tidy the crib,' said the vicar. 'Tomorrow is the Epiphany, so we have to add the last three figures, the wise men.'

'I always thought that they went to visit Jesus with the shepherds,' said David, one of the choirboys.

'That's what everyone seems to think,' replied the vicar. 'We should actually remember the wise men after Christmas at Epiphany, not at Christmas time.'

'But who were they? Sometimes we call them kings and sometimes wise men – which is right?' asked Andrew, the other choirboy.

'They were very clever men who had seen a bright star and who followed it all the way from Persia to Bethlehem. They believed that a bright star meant that a very important person had been born. Because this baby was to be so special they had brought presents with them. If you look carefully at our crib figures you can see what they are carrying.'

Maximus meanwhile had been crouching deep in the straw and was hoping that the tidying up wasn't going to include his hiding place. Just as he thought he was going to be discovered the vicar and the choirboys each put down a figure of a wise man close to the baby Jesus.

'I know,' said David, 'Gold, frankinstein and myrrh.'

'Well, not quite,' laughed the vicar. 'Actually it was

gold, frankincense and myrrh. Three very suitable gifts for Jesus.'

'They seem a bit odd to me,' said Andrew. 'I can understand the gold – but what are the other two?'

'At the time when Jesus lived gold was the king of metals, the most precious and expensive of all. The king of metals for the king of the world. Frankincense was used in worship – when it was burned it gave off smoke and a fragrant smell. The wise men knew that Jesus was someone to be worshipped. I wonder if you can spell myrrh?' the vicar asked the two boys.

'Yes, it's easy,' boasted David. 'M E R E'.

'Good try, but not quite right,' replied the vicar. 'It's actually M Y R R H. It was poured over the body of a person who had died before they were buried. Jesus was going to die thirty years later on the cross.'

'Gold for a king, frankincense for one we worship,' said Andrew.

'And myrrh for one who is to die,' added David.

'That's right,' said the vicar. 'But there is one other thing – the word Epiphany. It means 'showing forth'. You see Jesus was a Jew. The Jews had been waiting for a long time for a king to lead them. The wise men were not Jews – but they were amongst the first people to see Jesus. Jesus was and is so special that he is for everyone, not just the Jews. So at Epiphany we remember that Jesus was shown to the whole world – everyone everywhere can come to know and love him.'

Maximus stretched his cramped legs as the vicar and choirboys went off. Now he knew he was right – there had been something missing from the crib, and he ran off to the vestry without thinking any more about wax waffles.

Heavenly Father,
Thank you for the wise men who brought gifts to Jesus.
Help us to bring to him the gift of ourselves each day
and to remember that Jesus loves everyone, everywhere.
Amen

Maximus and harvest festival

For most Christians there are two days in the year which are especially important. One of these is Christmas when we remember the birth of Jesus and the other is Easter Day when we give thanks that Jesus is alive. Although Maximus lives in the church he is not always a very religious mouse and neither Christmas nor Easter are his special day. Maximus looks forward to harvest festival most of all. This may be because his great grandfather, Albert, was a fieldmouse.

As you know, Maximus is very fond of his food. In fact it is true to say that Maximus is a greedy mouse who eats far too much. There are even times when he has been stuck trying to get in and out of his front door hole in the vestry wall. He does sometimes try to lose weight by jogging round the organ or lifting a candle above his head five times a day. One day he even went to Weight Watchers Anonymouse. The real problem is that he loves his food and that is why he looks forward to harvest festival each year.

Normally of course Maximus lives on hymnburgers,

candle chips or biscuits left lying around the church after the toddlers' service. At harvest he knows that lots of people will bring fruit and vegetables just for him to eat. In fact they even play a game with him by putting the food all over the church.

It was the Harvest Festival Family Service and Maximus had hidden himself behind the curtain to watch. He saw the children take up lots of lovely food to the vicar and rubbed his tummy thinking of the feast he would have later. Then the vicar started to talk to the children and adults in the church.

'We have come here today to think about all the good things which we have. At harvest we thank God especially for all the food which is grown for us. Very few of us are hungry, in fact most of us have more to eat than we need. We praise God for all that he gives us. At the end of this service your kind gifts will be shared with those people who are not as fortunate as ourselves. And the money which you give today will be sent to help those in other countries who are trying hard to grow better crops to feed more of their people who are really starving.'

Maximus thought to himself – all this nice food is not for me after all. It's for others who are hungry. I always have enough – too much sometimes. Perhaps I ought to give some of this lovely food away. I wonder who needs it? I don't think Barnabas the bat can be hungry. Patrick and his mouse family in the Sunday School cupboard are fine. Johann Sebastian, the organist's cat, certainly doesn't need any. Harold the hedgehog has plenty. I know, what about Robert the rabbit and his family?

Robert and his new family lived in a burrow in the churchyard and helped to keep the grass short. Maximus

knew that with five children, Robert and Rebecca found it difficult to find enough food to feed them all. After the service Maximus collected some carrots and cabbages and put them by the church door. He went in search of Robert and Rebecca and saw them looking very worried.

'What ever is the matter?' asked Maximus.

'The church people need somewhere to park their cars. They are going to put a car park over most of our grass. We don't know how we can feed the children.'

Maximus explained to them about harvest festival, how people should share what they have with others who are hungry. They all went over to the church door and Robert and Rebecca took the carrots and cabbages to the family. I really must have a word with the vicar, thought Maximus. Perhaps the rabbits could eat the grass in his garden?

Heavenly Father,
You have given us so much. Help us, not only to be thankful, but to be willing to share with other people what you have given us. Amen

Maximus learns a lesson

Maximus was having his breakfast. He had found a very thick book full of stories about people who lived years ago, called saints. One chapter a day gave him a good breakfast and he called this his serial story. Just as he was nibbling the last few words of a story about St Pancras he heard a loud noise in the church. He ran quickly through the vestry door and had a look round. Just disappearing out of an open window he saw a large furry tail. It was Johann Sebastian, the organist's cat.

Maximus had never spoken to Johann Sebastian, in fact every time he saw him he scampered away as fast as his little paws could go, hoping the cat would not see him. Johann Sebastian knew all about churches, he had been brought up in a cathedral and had learnt his catechism as a young kitten. But Maximus did not know this and was very frightened of him.

The next Sunday, after the morning service, the vicar made the font ready for baptisms in the afternoon. He put water in the bowl and went off to have his lunch. Maximus was not very sure what happened at baptisms

and wondered what it was that the vicar poured over the babies. When the church was quiet he climbed up the legs of the font and stood looking into the basin. He stretched out one paw to taste whatever it was in the bowl. The metal bowl was slippery and before he knew it Maximus had tobogganed down the side. He fell into the water with a loud shout and splash.

Sad to say, Maximus had never learned how to swim when he was at school. On swimming days he didn't take his trunks or towel and he used to ask his mother to write notes to excuse him from swimming. So there he was, splashing around in the font, swallowing water and trying to shout 'help, help, help,' at the same time. The sides of the bowl were so steep and slippery that he could not get out.

It just so happened that as Maximus fell into the font, Johann Sebastian came in through the church window to get a piece of music for the organist. He heard the loud shout and splash but did not know where it came from. Johann Sebastian was a kind cat and did not want to leave anyone in trouble so he ran around the church listening. Maximus made one final effort to shout 'help'. Johann Sebastian realised where the noise was coming from and leapt up onto the font.

Just as Maximus was sinking for the last time Johann Sebastian stretched out a long furry paw and hoisted out a very wet and unhappy Maximus.

'What you need,' said Johann Sebastian, 'is mouse to mouse resuscitation. However, I'll wrap you up in this nice white cloth and you'll soon dry out and feel a lot better.'

After that near escape Maximus never ran away from Johann Sebastian again. They became good friends and Maximus realised that he should not judge others before he got to know them.

Heavenly Father,
Help us to get to know people properly before we judge
them. Thank you for our friends and for all who help
us. Amen

Maximus in the swim

'I'll never do it,' shouted Maximus to Patrick. 'I just can't. Every time I try, I keep sinking and swallowing gallons of water. If mice had been meant to swim they would have been given fins.'

Ever since Maximus had fallen into the font and been rescued from drowning by Johann Sebastian, the organist's cat, Patrick had been determined to teach his friend to swim. He had made Maximus lie down over a hymn book and coached him in the breast stroke. Maximus happily kicked his little paws out and back on dry land but as soon as he got anywhere near the water he forgot all that Patrick had told him and panicked.

'I really don't know why I have so much trouble with you!' said Patrick. 'Paula and I have taught all our little ones to swim. Percival won the two metre front crawl at school and Pauline came second in the five metre back stroke. Here's you, a big grown up mouse, who won't even try – you should be ashamed of yourself.' And with that Patrick stormed out of the vestry and went back to his home in the Sunday School cupboard.

Maximus decided that he really ought to go out and do some shopping. He had run out of Maxwell Mouse coffee and needed several other things as well. He put on his coat, took out his shopping bag, and set off down the road. The Supermarket was a good walk away and Maximus usually went through the park as he liked to talk to the ducks on the pond. As he was passing the swings and roundabouts, which were next to the pond, he heard a splash and a shout. He rushed over to the edge of the pond and just saw a little prickly head go under the water. It came up with a lot more noise and then went under the surface again.

Maximus recognised Henrietta, Herbert the hedgehog's youngest daughter, as she rose to the top once more. For a moment Maximus didn't know what to do. There was no time to 'phone the police – Henrietta would have drowned long before they arrived. There was no one else about in the park. He could shout for help but, with the traffic on the road, he would never be heard.

Then, without thinking about it, Maximus tore off his coat, threw off his shoes, and jumped in. He had forgotten all his own fears about the water and was only thinking about Henrietta. Swimming seemed to come quite naturally to him after all Patrick's lessons. He swam quickly over to where he had last seen the baby hedgehog. Taking a deep breath, he ducked his head under the water. Just below him were a lot of bubbles. He made himself swim down and managed to grab one of Henrietta's front paws. Kicking and spluttering Maximus forced his way to the surface. After a great struggle he managed to pull the half drowned baby hedgehog towards the side. By the time he got there Herbert, Henrietta's father, was jumping up and down on the edge and shouting at him.

'Come on, Maximus, only another few feet,' yelled Herbert, who was stretching so far out that he was in danger of falling in himself. 'Oh, Maximus, that was so brave. Thank you, thank you, thank you.'

'Just help me out of here,' begged Maximus. 'I'm freezing to death in this water.' Herbert took his baby daughter from Maximus and gently put her on the ground. Then with a great heave he lifted Maximus onto the side.

'Faith,' said the vicar next Sunday morning, 'is trusting in something or someone you cannot see. Faith in God means believing that Jesus is alive and loves us even if we cannot see him.'

'It's a bit like me swimming,' muttered Maximus to himself. 'I couldn't see anything in the water holding me up but it did it all right.' And he went off after church to a special Thank You party for him at Herbert's house.

Heavenly Father,
Help us to believe and trust in you, for even though we cannot see you, you are always there surrounding us with your love. Amen

Maximus loses his temper

It was not a good day for Maximus. First of all he had not slept well the night before. He had eaten a very dusty hymnburger. He had found an old hymnbook behind the organ which must have been there for years and years. After he had eaten it he had bad tummy ache all night, but that was not the only problem. His hanky duvet had holes in it where he had nibbled away for the past few nights and he woke up feeling very cold with his paws sticking out through one of the holes.

He had been expecting a letter in the post from his cousin Chrismus. He had been hoping for an invitation to stay with Chrismus for a short holiday but no letter had come. Maximus still felt ill and did not want any breakfast. In fact Maximus was very cross with the world.

'I'm fed up, fed up, fed up!' he shouted as he stumped down the aisle of the church. 'Nobody cares about me, nobody cares that I've got tummy ache,' he grumbled. 'I spend all my time looking after the church, but does anyone look after me? No, of course they don't. I might as well go and find a proper mousehole of my own.'

Just at that moment Barnabas, the bat who lived in the belfry, came swooping down, flapping his wings and causing quite a wind.

'Go away, you beastly bat,' shouted Maximus. 'Can't you see I've got tummy ache? All you bats do is frighten respectable mice by your low flying. Don't you know there is a law against low flying bats in churches?'

'You've really got the miseries today,' said Barnabas. 'Misery mouse, that's what you are. Just a misery mouse.'

Patrick had heard all the noise in the church and came scampering out to see what had happened. He skidded on the newly polished church tiles and crashed into Maximus.

'Can't you mind where you're going?' shouted Maximus angrily.

'Here I am minding my own tummy ache, not disturbing anyone, when first I'm attacked by a dive bombing bat and then by a crazy mouse who thinks he's a Grand Prix driver. I thought churches were supposed to be places of peace and quiet. Fat chance of finding any here with you two about.'

Maximus turned round and tried to look very fierce as he walked slowly back to the vestry. He could hear Barnabas and Patrick talking to each other behind his back.

'Poor old Maximus,' said Barnabas to Patrick. 'He's usually a good tempered mouse.'

'Yes, I think we shall have to do something to cheer him up,' replied Patrick. 'I've got an idea.'

The two creatures went down to the back of the church and whispered to each other. In a few moments Barnabas flew back to the belfry and Patrick disappeared into the Sunday School cupboard.

At about three o'clock Maximus, who had fallen asleep in the vestry, was woken by a knocking sound. He tumbled out of bed and grumpily opened the door.

'What is it now?' he started to say, and then stopped in surprise. Standing at the door were two of the strangest looking beings he had ever seen. Barnabas was wearing a mask on his face and a cloak over his wings. Patrick also had a cloak on, made from an old handkerchief, and a paper bag mask.

'Enter Batman and Patrick the Mouse Wonder!' said Barnabas.

'We've come to cheer you up,' said Patrick. 'We fight all the things that make mice bad tempered.'

By this time Maximus was laughing so much that he could not speak. They just looked so funny, Barnabas's wings were sticking out through his cloak and Patrick's whiskers were caught up in his mask making him sneeze. Maximus just lay down on the floor and rolled around clutching his tummy and laughed and laughed and laughed.

Later on, after a special tea party, Maximus thanked his two friends for making him happy again. He told them he was sorry for being so bad tempered.

Heavenly Father,
Forgive us when we are bad tempered and selfish. Help us to remember how much you have given us and to be thankful. Amen

Maximus learns the truth

'Well I never. I've never noticed that before. How very odd,' Maximus muttered to himself. It was a Monday morning and Maximus had done his washing and was hanging it out to dry around the church boiler.

There was his night shirt and his day shirt, seven pairs of socks, three pairs of jeans and his underwear. As he hung up a striped pair of pants in his favourite team colours, those of Mousehampton United, he noticed something very strange. Round the elastic waist band he could see a name he knew. He looked at all his clothes. They all had the same name on them. Not only that, it was the same name as the church where Maximus lived. Maximus ran off to the Sunday School cupboard to find Patrick and his wife and their forty-seven, or was it forty-eight, children?

'You'll never guess what I've discovered,' he panted as he burst in on them having a late breakfast. 'The vicar makes clothes and sells them in big shops. He must make lots and lots of money. Some people are so greedy – because he's always asking us for even more

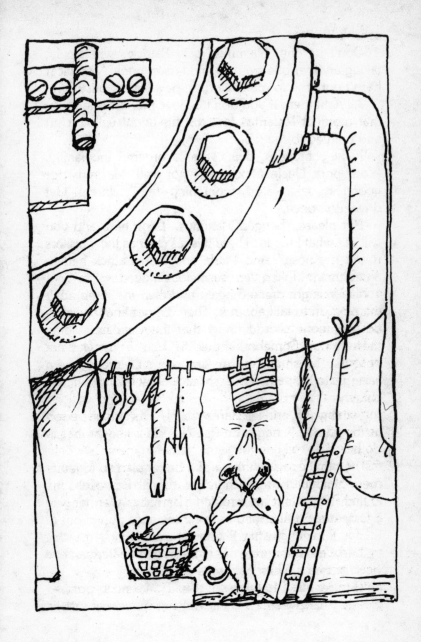

as well.'

'Don't be daft, Maximus,' said Patrick's wife Paula, taking another bite from an old lesson book. 'The vicar hasn't got time to make clothes, he's far too busy.'

'All right then, if you don't believe me, look here.' At that moment Maximus took off his bright yellow shirt and pointed to the label.

'Hide your eyes, dears,' Paula ordered the family. 'Your poor Uncle Maximus is not well. Maximus, for goodness sake, stop frightening the children. Get dressed at once.'

'But please,' begged Maximus. 'Look here and you will see what I mean. There it is, as clear as the whiskers round my nose.' And Paula and then Patrick had to agree that it looked very suspicious indeed.

Maximus got dressed again and then the three adult mice began to talk about it. They did not know what to do. Someone should know that the vicar was doing these things. Someone should be told. It just was not right that he should be making so much money from selling clothes when he should be working for the church.

'I vote we go and tell Barnabas. He's the wisest person in the church,' suggested Patrick. 'He'll know what to do.'

The others couldn't think of a better plan so together they climbed the church tower to tell Barnabas, the church bat, about the problem. Barnabas was hanging upside down fast asleep as the three mice puffed out of breath into the belfry. Barnabas slept during the day and flew around during the night so that he kept an eye on the church whilst Maximus was asleep.

'Excuse me, Barnabas,' asked Maximus politely. Nothing happened. The bat did not move but just let out another gentle snore. Just then there was a very loud whirring sound followed by ten ear shattering bongs. The mice were terrified. The bat did not stir.

'Excuse me, Barnabas,' whispered Maximus again after the noise had died down. The bat stirred and opened one eye.

'Yes, what is it? Why are you up here shouting at me? Can't a bat get an honest day's sleep in peace?'

'We need your help,' said Paula with more courage than the other two. 'We have a problem which we think you should know about.'

'Problem?' asked Barnabas with a yawn. 'Then go to the vicar. He's good at finding answers to problems.'

'. . . er, we can't go to the vicar,' muttered Patrick. 'He is the problem!' Between them they told Barnabas, who had now quite woken up, what Maximus had discovered. The vicar was obviously making and selling clothes and putting the name of the church on them. They told the bat how shocked they were and how they felt they should tell somebody important what was going on.

'Well, you three had better thank your lucky stars you came to see me before telling anyone else,' replied the bat sternly. 'You really have got the wrong end of the stick this time. Now listen, and listen hard. The vicar does not make clothes to sell in big shops. You, Maximus, bought all your clothes from one shop and it is their name on the label, 'St. Michael'. It just happens to be the same name as our church.'

'Oh dear,' said Maximus. 'I've got it wrong again.'

'Indeed you have. Just be quite sure about the facts before you go around spreading untrue gossip and rumours about people. You must think before you speak. Now let me catch up with my batty sleep,' said the bat, shutting both eyes.

Before the three mice had left the belfry the bat was fast asleep.

Heavenly Father,
It is very easy to hurt other people by gossiping about
them. Help us only to speak of others when we have
nice things to say. Amen

Not everything is grey

'The trouble with foreigners,' said Maximus to Patrick, 'is that they speak foreign.' The two mice had been having a long discussion about holidays. Maximus had never been abroad for his holidays – he had stayed with various relations from time to time, but unlike Patrick and his family, he had never left England.

'Of course they do,' laughed Patrick. 'To them you speak foreign too! Just because a mouse doesn't speak the same language as you, or eat the same food . . .'

'Yes, that's another thing,' interrupted Maximus. 'All that horrible smelly cheese . . . blue with little worms crawling in and out of it. Or what's that other one – all full of holes? Why pay for cheese with holes in it, I ask you? It only goes to show what foreign mice are like.'

'Maximus, you are so wrong,' argued Patrick. 'If you would only go and see for yourself. We had a really great holiday last year in Miceland – the weather was hot, the food was good, and most of all the mice were really friendly. Most of them speak English. Just as well, since so few English mice speak any foreign languages at all.'

'No, it's just not right,' replied Maximus. 'As far as I'm concerned we grey mice are different from those foreign white mice. They should all learn to speak proper English and eat decent food. We should keep to ourselves. All those foreign mice coming over here and taking our jobs. I bet if you went to some of our churches you would find a white mouse looking after them. Those white mice are getting everywhere.'

'But they are exactly the same as us!' exploded Patrick. 'They may be a different colour and speak another language but they are the same as you and me.'

'Sorry, Patrick, but I think you're wrong,' said Maximus. And he turned away from his friend and scampered off to look for some lunch, muttering to himself as he went. 'White mice indeed – it's just not natural. Proper mice are grey – not blooming white.'

It was not the first time that Patrick and Maximus had argued over grey and white mice. Patrick had tried hard to make Maximus understand that white mice were just as normal mice as grey ones – that the only difference was their colour. He never seemed to get anywhere – Maximus's mind was made up and he wouldn't listen to anyone else.

Just as Patrick was going back to join the family in the Sunday School cupboard he heard a loud bang. This was followed by a shout from somewhere in the church. Patrick ran, as fast as his short legs could manage, towards the noise. Just by the pulpit he saw something very odd. It was a large book lying on the floor moving up and down and making a groaning noise as it did so. Patrick investigated further. He lifted the corner of the book just as it rose silently in the air. Underneath was a very unhappy looking Maximus.

'I think I've broken my leg!', moaned Maximus. 'I climbed the pulpit to get a bite of the Vicar's sermon notes and fell off. Then his hymn book fell on top of me. I shall never be the same again.'

Patrick heaved the heavy book up from Maximus and took a close look at his friend. He did indeed seem to have hurt his leg quite badly.

'I'm going to 'phone for the doctor. He will decide what to do about your leg. You may have to go to hospital.'

After about a quarter of an hour the church door opened and in came a mouse wearing a black suit and carrying a big black bag. Patrick, who had been waiting for the doctor near the back of the church, gave a gasp. The doctor was a white mouse, not their usual doctor who was grey like them.

'Now what seems to be the trouble?' said the doctor in perfect English. 'It's Mr. Maximus, isn't it?'

'Yes,' stuttered Maximus, looking up at the doctor. 'I fell from the pulpit and I think I've broken my leg.'

The white mouse felt the leg very gently and asked Maximus to bend it and wiggle it about a bit.

'No,' said the doctor with a smile. 'You have been lucky this time. It is badly bruised and you will have to be careful for several days — but it isn't broken. Now off to bed for a lie down. I will come and see you again in a few days.'

The doctor picked up his bag and went out of the Church. Patrick helped Maximus back to the vestry and into bed.

'There you are,' he said. 'You are a real fraud! You didn't mind a white mouse doctor helping you when you needed it, did you?'

'No, you're right, Patrick. He was very kind. I expect

all white mice are like that really – just the same as us.'
And Maximus thought a lot more about it as his leg got
better.

Heavenly Father,
We often think wrong things about people we don't
really know. Forgive us and help us to understand that
we can learn much from each other. Amen

Maximus is jealous

'It's just not fair,' stormed Maximus. 'It's not as if he's been here half as long as me. In fact if it wasn't for me he wouldn't be here at all. I let him in, looked after him, suggested he and his family had the Sunday School cupboard. And how does he repay my kindness? By being chosen for the Family Service. Not me who looks after the church. Not me who is always here. It's just not fair.'

Maximus was shouting at the vestry wall. He was in a real mood. He kicked the door and then hopped around trying to hold his bruised front paws with his back paws. All he managed was to fall over in a heap on the floor. He lay there for a few minutes muttering to himself.

What had upset Maximus was the next Family Service. Once a month there was a special service at St. Michael's for all the children and young people. They sang choruses and modern hymns and there was always a really exciting talk. The vicar had announced that the next one would be an Animal Service. Any children who had pets were invited to bring them to the church. Maximus heard all about this from the choirboys and girls. They were discussing, one Sunday morning after the service, what animals they might bring.

'I'm going to bring Smudgie, my spaniel,' said Ann. 'I hope he doesn't fight with your cat, Jackie.'

'She'd chase your dog out of the church,' boasted Jackie.

'Not likely, Smudgie would see her off, dead quick,' replied Ann. 'Your rotten cat wouldn't stand a chance!'

'Oh, shut up, you two,' interrupted Andrew. 'Who wants to hear about your doggie and moggie? I shall bring Roland, my rat. I bet you two will scream and jump on the seats.'

'Take more than your smelly rat to make me do that,' said Jackie. 'My Tiger will soon make a meal out of Roland. Can't wait to see it – real wicked.'

'I hear the vicar is bringing the mouse who lives in the Sunday School cupboard,' added David. 'I suppose the organist will bring Johann Sebastian as well. Should be great.'

And that was what had upset Maximus. After all these years of hard work for the church he felt really upset that the vicar had chosen Patrick instead of him. Why should Patrick be chosen and get all the fame? It just wasn't fair and Maximus was very jealous. He refused to speak to Patrick for the two weeks before the Animal Service. Poor Patrick didn't know what he had done wrong as nobody had told him what was going to happen. He couldn't understand at all why Maximus was ignoring him.

The day of the Animal Service arrived and everyone was getting very excited – all that is, apart from Maximus, who was in the middle of a super sulk. He had been moping about with a scowl on his face for days. Not a very nice mouse to know at all.

One by one the children began to arrive with their animals. There were goldfish in gleaming glass bowls, cats in wicker baskets, dogs on leads, frogs in cardboard boxes, guinea pigs, mice, rats and budgies in cages, and one girl came on a pony which she had to leave outside the church. There were white rabbits, a talking parrot which said 'Hello George' all the time, an owl with a broken wing and even a baby hedgehog which had been rescued from being run over. Patrick was perched on the vicar's shoulder.

The vicar started the service and everyone sang 'All things bright and beautiful'. The parrot added a chorus of 'Hello George' at the end of every verse and one of the dogs started to growl at a black and white cat on the seat in front. During the prayers the animals were very quiet. 'This is a special service today,' announced the vicar. 'But then I don't really need to tell you that. It is really good to see so many animals with so many people and I am very pleased that Patrick let me come with him.'

At this, Maximus, who was listening at the vestry door, nearly burst a blood vessel. He was so cross that he was tempted to pack his suitcase and leave the church there and then. Fortunately he stayed just long enough to hear the next words.

'This is a special day because it is the first time we have had an Animal Service. But it is also a special day for another very important reason. On this day, two years ago, a small furry friend came to this church. During the past two years he has become very well known for all sorts of reasons. He cleans up, he tidies round, he guards the church, he makes friends with

everyone. Today we want to say a big thank you to Maximus, our church mouse. I know he's hiding at the vestry door and now I'm going to invite him to be the guest of honour at our first Animal Service.'

Andrew put down his hamster and brought Maximus to the vicar. Everyone clapped loudly as he was presented with a large slice of gift wrapped cheese. Maximus was a very happy mouse but he did feel rather ashamed about feeling so jealous of Patrick. After the service he ran over to the Sunday School cupboard and told Patrick how sorry he was and then shared his cheese with Patrick and Paula and the family.

Heavenly Father,
There are times when we get very jealous over the success of others. Help us to understand that we must do what we are able to do and not complain about what we cannot do. Amen